# The Littlest Matryoshka

CORINNE DEMAS BLISS

*Illustrated by* KATHRYN BROWN

𝒟𝒾𝓈𝓃ℰ𝓎 • Hyperion

Los Angeles New York

FIRST EDITION, September 1999
20  19
FAC-029191-19067
Printed in Malaysia

*LIBRARY OF CONGRESS CATALOGING-IN-PUBLICATION DATA*
Bliss, Corinne Demas.
The littlest matryoshka/by Corinne Demas Bliss: illustrated by Kathryn Brown.—1st ed.
p. cm.
Summary: Nina, the smallest of a group of Russian nesting dolls, is separated from her sisters
and swept along on a dangerous journey that eventually brings her back home.
ISBN 0-7868-0153-0 (trade).—ISBN 0-7868-2125-6 (library)
[1. Nesting dolls—Fiction. 2. Dolls—Fiction. 3. Lost and found possessions—Fiction.]
1. Brown, Kathryn, 1955- ill. II. Title.
PZ7.B61917Li 1999
[E]-dc21 94—43188

For Temi and Hadley and Elaine,
who all know the magic of matryoshkas
—*C. D. B.*

For Shelley, Rhonda, and Bobbi.
And for sisters everywhere.
—*K. B.*

In a small shop in a snowy village in Russia, Nikolai the doll maker was carving his last matryoshka. From one piece of soft wood he shaped six nesting dolls, each one fitting inside the other. They all opened in the middle and were hollow inside, except for the littlest. She was the size of a bumblebee, and she was made of the heart of the sweet-smelling wood.

Nikolai painted each doll's black shining hair and black shining eyes. He painted each doll's red dress and yellow shawl. He painted a fancy flower on the front of each doll's white apron and a smile on each doll's face.

"You are six sisters," he said, as he set them along the workbench in a line, from biggest to littlest. And he named each one, touching his finger to the top of her head: Anna, Olga, Varka, Vanda, Nadia, and Nina. Then he tucked them one inside the other.

He put Nina inside Nadia,
and Nadia inside Vanda,
and Vanda inside Varka,
and Varka inside Olga,
and Olga inside Anna.

Anna had a pedestal base, so she could not fit inside any other doll. She had the fanciest flower on the front of her apron, and the wisest look in her eyes.

"Good-bye, Anna," said Nikolai, and he kissed her forehead. "Keep your sisters safe inside you and may you find a happy home."

Then he sent the matryoshka off to a toy shop in America.

On the long journey across the sea Nina slept inside Nadia,

and Nadia slept inside Vanda,

and Vanda slept inside Varka,

and Varka slept inside Olga,

and Olga slept inside Anna.

Anna kept her shining eyes wide open.

She saw only darkness until she was unpacked from her box at a toy shop in America. There were other matryoshkas on the shelf by the front door. Some were bigger and some were smaller. Anna could only guess how many sisters they each held inside. Other matryoshka makers carved four or eight or even ten dolls each inside the other, but Nikolai always carved six, for six, he believed, was a lucky number.

The toy shop owner opened up Anna and set her and all her sisters in a line, from biggest to littlest, along the front of the display. Nina, the littlest, was on the very end of the shelf, too close to the edge.

One March day, the very end of winter, a shopper in a puffy coat brushed against the shelf and Nina was knocked right off. No one noticed except for Nina's sisters, but there was nothing they could do. They could not lift their painted arms to reach out for Nina or open their painted lips to cry for help.

Nina rolled to the doorway of the shop and then, in the bustle, she was kicked outside by a customer as he left. It had begun snowing, and soon Nina was covered up by snow.

In the morning the shopkeeper shoveled the sidewalk in front of the toy shop. Nina was shoveled right out to the street. Later that day, the snowplow came and pushed all the snow into a pile. The pile was shoveled up into a dump truck. Nina, nestled in the snow, saw only whiteness. The muffled sound of the truck reminded her of the ship's engine, and she dreamed she was on the sea again, on her way to America. The truck dumped all the snow on top of a big pile outside of town.

That evening the shopkeeper discovered that the littlest matryoshka was missing. He looked everywhere, but couldn't find her.

So he put Nadia inside Vanda,

and Vanda inside Varka,

and Varka inside Olga,

and Olga inside Anna.

And he put the matryoshka on the sale table.

The next day a little girl named Jessie came to the toy shop with the money her grandfather had sent for her birthday. She had seen the matryoshkas on display in the store weeks before and longed for one. But now she found out they were all too expensive. She was just turning away when the shopkeeper pointed out Anna.

"The littlest doll is missing," said the shopkeeper, "so I'll let you have that matryoshka for half-price."

Jessie had just enough money to buy the matryoshka.

When she got home she set the dolls along her dresser in a line, from biggest to littlest. At night she put a little ball of cotton inside Nadia, so she wouldn't feel empty inside.

Then she put Nadia inside Vanda,

and Vanda inside Varka,

and Varka inside Olga,

and Olga inside Anna.

And she set Anna by the window so she could look out at the moonlit, snowy fields and the star-filled sky. Anna kept her shining eyes wide open, watching for Nina and remembering Nikolai's soft voice:

*"Keep your sisters safe inside you."*

Nina spent the night in the snow pile. In the quiet of early morning, spring took the place of winter. The sun came out, and the great thaw began. The snow above Nina started melting, and soon she could see sunlight making its way through the icy crystals. By the next afternoon, all the snow around Nina had melted away. For a while she lay in a little puddle, in a pocket of snow. When that melted, she was carried along in a rivulet of melted snow down the hillside to a stream.

Nina rolled and tumbled along in the current. She had glimpses of the sky and glimpses of the sandy bottom and glimpses of the rocks she whooshed past. A roar in the distance got louder and louder. It wasn't a truck or the engine of a ship. It was a waterfall. Suddenly Nina was caught in a rush of water, and then she flew off into space and came down in foaming surf. She was pounded deep in the water but popped up and was carried off downstream once again.

The stream widened and branched in two. Nina traveled up one fork to an inlet. She floated gently along in the slow current. A great blue heron, back from the south now that the ice had melted, was hunting in the shallows. He spotted Nina and snapped her up. When he discovered she wasn't anything to eat he flicked her away.

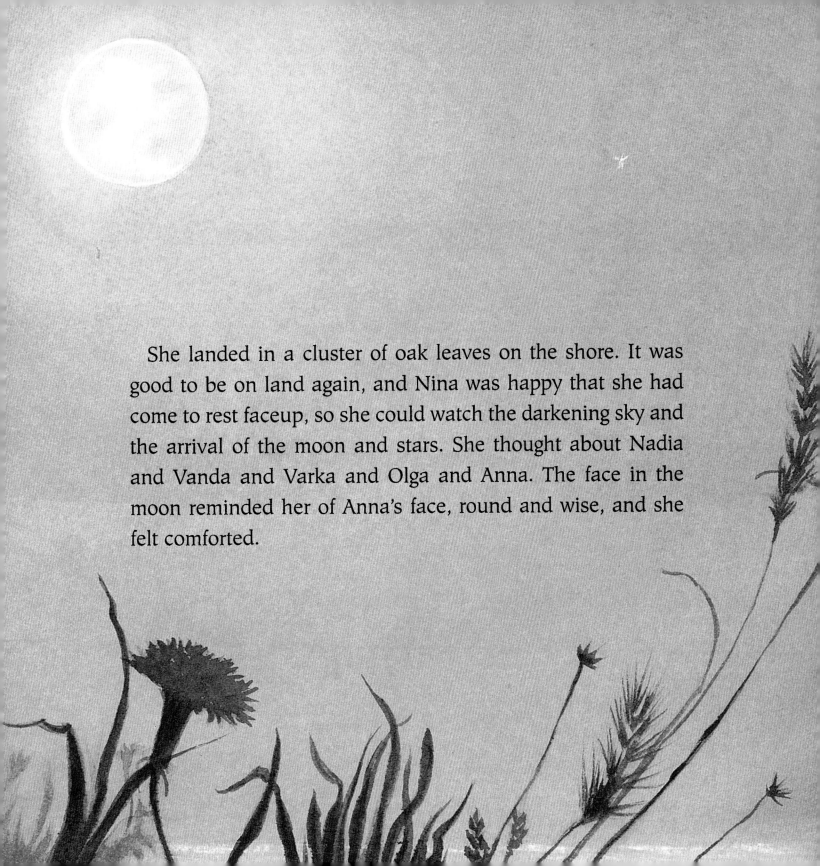

She landed in a cluster of oak leaves on the shore. It was good to be on land again, and Nina was happy that she had come to rest faceup, so she could watch the darkening sky and the arrival of the moon and stars. She thought about Nadia and Vanda and Varka and Olga and Anna. The face in the moon reminded her of Anna's face, round and wise, and she felt comforted.

In the morning a squirrel came foraging among the leaves. He mistook her for a nut, snatched her up, and dashed off with her to his nest in the eaves of an attic. When he saw that she was only a piece of wood, he shoved her out of the nest and she fell to the roof of the porch below. She rolled down the slope of the roof, into the rain gutter, and then tumbled down the copper drainpipe.

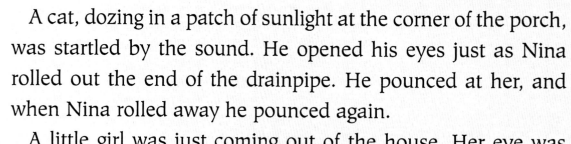

A cat, dozing in a patch of sunlight at the corner of the porch, was startled by the sound. He opened his eyes just as Nina rolled out the end of the drainpipe. He pounced at her, and when Nina rolled away he pounced again.

A little girl was just coming out of the house. Her eye was caught by the red of Nina's dress.

"What have you got there?" she asked the cat as she bent down to look. She picked up the littlest matryoshka.

"Oh, you found us!" she cried, for the little girl was Jessie. She ran upstairs to her bedroom. She wiped Nina carefully with a handkerchief and placed her in a circle with her sisters, so Nina could see them all and they could all see her. How they rejoiced to be together again!

That night Jessie removed the cotton ball from Nadia.

She put Nina inside Nadia,

and Nadia inside Vanda,

and Vanda inside Varka,

and Varka inside Olga,

and Olga inside Anna.

"Now your sisters are safe inside you," Jessie said, and she kissed Anna on her forehead. Anna smiled the smile that had been painted on by Nikolai the doll maker in Russia, so long ago.

# Author's Note

The first nesting dolls were made in China in the early 1800s, where the tradition of nesting boxes had been started hundreds of years earlier. The idea came to Russia in the 1890s, when a group of artists was reviving native culture and folk traditions. One artist, Sergei Malyutin, probably inspired by a Japanese example, designed the first set of Russian nesting dolls, the largest, a peasant girl with a *babushka* (kerchief) on her head. The dolls were carved and turned on the lathe by a master wood-carver, then painted. This first matryoshka was the inspiration for the folk artists in Semonov (a Russian town near the city of Gorky), a region where the most traditional matryoshkas—like the one in this story—are still made. Many regions of Russia took up the art, each developing a particular style. Most of the dolls are maidens, but some sets have families, characters (like St. Nick), or animals.

The Russian word *matpёwka* is spelled in English three ways: matryoshka, matrioshka, and matreshka. (The Russian letter *E* is pronounced "yo.") The word comes from the common peasant female name *Matryona*, which is derived from the word for "mother," and the dolls have been a symbol for motherhood and fertility.

Nesting dolls are made in many countries now, including India, Poland, Japan, and China, but the Russian matryoshkas are still the best known.